Dear Parents:

Congratulations! Your child is taking the first steps on an exciting journey. The destination? Independent reading!

STEP INTO READING® will help your child get there. The program offers five steps to reading success. Each step includes fun stories and colorful art or photographs. In addition to original fiction and books with favorite characters, there are Step into Reading Non-Fiction Readers, Phonics Readers and Boxed Sets, Sticker Readers, and Comic Readers—a complete literacy program with something to interest every child.

Learning to Read, Step by Step!

Ready to Read   Preschool–Kindergarten
• big type and easy words • rhyme and rhythm • picture clues
For children who know the alphabet and are eager to begin reading.

Reading with Help   Preschool–Grade 1
• basic vocabulary • short sentences • simple stories
For children who recognize familiar words and sound out new words with help.

Reading on Your Own   Grades 1–3
• engaging characters • easy-to-follow plots • popular topics
For children who are ready to read on their own.

Reading Paragraphs   Grades 2–3
• challenging vocabulary • short paragraphs • exciting stories
For newly independent readers who read simple sentences with confidence.

Ready for Chapters   Grades 2–4
• chapters • longer paragraphs • full-color art
For children who want to take the plunge into chapter books but still like colorful pictures.

STEP INTO READING® is designed to give every child a successful reading experience. The grade levels are only guides; children will progress through the steps at their own speed, developing confidence in their reading.

Remember, a lifetime love of reading starts with a single step!

Visit us on the Web!
StepIntoReading.com
rhcbooks.com

Educators and librarians, for a variety of teaching tools, visit us at RHTeachersLibrarians.com

ISBN 978-0-593-57102-6 (trade) — ISBN 978-0-593-57103-3 (lib. bdg.)
ISBN 978-0-593-57104-0 (ebook)

Printed in the United States of America

10 9 8 7 6 5 4 3 2 1

SNOOZING SUN

by JohnTom Knight

Random House 🏠 New York

Kodi, Summer, and Eddy
are Junior Park Rangers.
They say hello to
DeeDee!

DeeDee is excited

for sunset.

But the sun

is not setting.

Lizard says Spirit Park
needs help.
The kids know
what to do!

The kids transform
into their
Spirit forms.

Let's go, Spirit Rangers!

The Spirit Rangers
are in Spirit Park.
They look for
the Chumash
Sun Spirit, Sunny.

Sunny is sleeping
on the mountain.
He is snoring, too!

Coyote wants
Sunny to leave.
It should be
nighttime!

Kodi knows who can
wake up Sunny!

Condor is the strongest
bird in Spirit Park.
He can wake up Sunny!

But he does not want
to burn his feathers.
He thinks they make him
look like a hero.

Summer Hawk picks up
Eddy Turtle.
They fly up high.
Eddy Turtle tosses
a water bubble at Sunny.

The water

turns to steam!

Sunny is too hot.

New plan!

The rangers use

a lasso.

They tug on Sunny.

Uh-oh!
Sunny is rolling down
the mountain!

Kodi holds Sunny up.

But Kodi needs help!

His fur is getting burned!

Condor to the rescue!
He lifts Sunny back
into the sky.

The day is saved!
But Condor's feathers
are burned.

Condor loves
his new look!
Now he knows that
your heart is what
makes you a hero.

Great job, Spirit Rangers!